THE

TALE

OF

PARADISE

LOST

The Tale of
PARADISE
LOST

Based on the poem
by John Milton
told as the story of the war
in Heaven,
the disobedience
of Adam and Eve,
and
their exit from Eden
into the world

retold by nancy willard and illustrated by jude daly

Atheneum Books for Young Readers

New York London Toronto Sydney

Atheneum Books for Young Readers

An imprint of Simon & Schuster

Children's Publishing Division

1230 Avenue of the Americas

New York, New York 10020

The excerpt on p. 147 is from *Paradise Lost*

by John Milton, edited by Merritt Y. Hughes

(New York: The Odyssey Press, Inc., 1935).

Book design by Ann Bobco

The text of this book is set in Golden Cockerel.

The illustrations are rendered in watercolor.

Manufactured in China

First Edition

10 9 8 7 6 5 4 3 2 1

Library of Congress Cataloging-in-

Publication Data

Willard, Nancy.

The tale of paradise lost: based on the poem

by John Milton. / Nancy Willard ; illustrated

by Jude Daly.—1st ed.

p.   cm.

Summary: A prose retelling of John Milton's

narrative poem chronicling the war in heaven

between competing angels and how the

disobedience of Adam and Eve led to their

expulsion from the Garden of Eden.

ISBN 0-689-85097-2

1. Adam (Biblical figure)—Juvenile fiction.

2. Eve (Biblical figure)—Juvenile fiction.

[1. Adam (Biblical figure)—Fiction. 2. Eve

(Biblical figure)—Fiction. 3. Milton, John,

1608–1674. Paradise lost—Adaptations.]

I. Milton, John, 1608–1674. Paradise lost.

II. Daly, Jude, ill. III. Title.

PZ7.W6553 Tal 2004

[Fic]—dc22   2003060083

For James Anatole
—N. W.

For Laura Cecil
—J. D.

THE WRITER TO THE READER

READER: When did you first hear the story of Adam and Eve and the serpent in the Garden of Eden?

WRITER: For me, that story is like one of those family stories you've heard so often and from so many different people you can't possibly remember your first encounter with it. I could tell you how my grandfather liked to quiz his grandchildren on the Bible because he thought it was a book we should know. I could tell you how my mother sent my sister and me to an after-school Bible class because she thought it was a book we should know.

How could I not be aware of that story? I remember a diner which featured on its menu "Adam and Eve on a raft," which turned out to be an exciting name for scrambled eggs on toast. Bits and pieces of the story popped up in the strangest places.

Not until I went to college did I read *Paradise Lost.*

READER: So why did you decide to retell Milton's epic poem as a story?

WRITER: I wanted to write a book that would invite younger readers into the tale. And I knew that retelling *Paradise Lost* and keeping as much of Milton's imagery as possible would take me on a long journey.

May the readers of this book have the pleasure of discovering the astonishing poem that inspired it.

Note: When *Paradise Lost* was begun in 1656, Milton had already lost his sight. In my mind's eye I see him rising each morning and dictating the poem, line by line, to his two daughters. It was originally published in 1667, and reprinted, with Milton's revisions, in 1674.

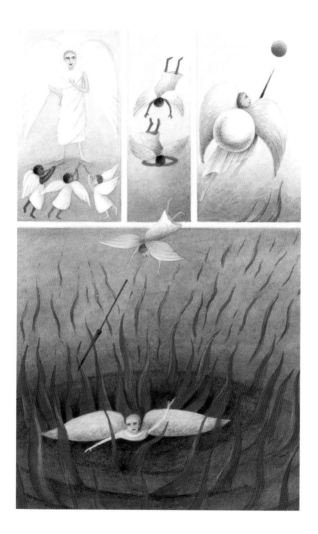

ONE

Long, long ago, before the world was, before minutes ticked and seconds tocked, before beginnings had endings, there was a war in Heaven. The most radiant of God's angels was also the most proud. "Why shouldn't I rule Heaven?" he asked himself, and he raised an army against God. One third of the angels in Heaven followed him. For three days they fought, and on the third day God hurled the whole lot of them out of Heaven, headlong into the bottomless dark of Hell.

Nine days and nine nights they fell. Their radiance vanished, and their names were no longer spoken in Heaven. Now they carried new names: Beelzebub and Mammon and Azazel and Mulciber.

The name of their leader was Satan.

Now let me tell you about the place God prepared for them. All around them roared floods of fire and whirlwinds of flame that gave no light but made the darkness darker. And there, big as a whale, stretched out on the burning lake, lay Satan. He turned to Beelzebub, his second in command. With the light of Heaven snuffed out of Beelzebub, Satan hardly recognized him.

"All is not lost," said Satan. "We still have the power of our hatred. I shall never bow before the Lord."

"Oh, Prince and Chief, what if God left us our courage only to make us suffer more?"

Satan lifted his head, and the flames rolled and billowed around him.

"Better to reign in Hell than to serve in Heaven. Hail horrors! Receive your new ruler. Let us fly to that bare stretch of land and lay plans to overcome this calamity."

He reared up, stretched his wings, flew through the stench and the darkness, and alighted on the burning plain, with Beelzebub close behind. The rest of their army lay groveling on the Lake of Fire, scattered like autumn leaves.

"When they hear your voice," said Beelzebub, "they will take heart and find new courage."

The earth singed his feet as Satan strode toward the shore. His massive shield hung shining on his shoulders like the moon, and he raised a spear as tall as the mast of a ship. Now he stood on the brimstone at the edge of that burning sea and called out, "Princes, warriors, have you surrendered? Even here God's angels can pin us with thunderbolts to the bottom of this pit. Stand up or stay fallen forever."

Up sprang the angels, as if they'd fallen asleep on duty. Satan lifted his spear and directed them to take their places on the brimstone. Then he commanded the trumpets to sound.

The warrior Azazel unfurled a flag emblazoned in gold and jewels, which streamed in the wind like a meteor. And now ten thousand banners filled the air and a forest of spears and helmets glittered over a wall of shields too vast to count, and above all this towered Satan, an archangel in ruins, though he kept a little of his old brightness.

"Now we know God's might. So let us work in secret by trickery and fraud. I have heard that God plans to make a new world. Our task is to make God's world fail. Let us rally our forces!"

At Satan's words, a million fallen angels drew their swords, and the flash of their blades lit that dark place, and the clang of swords on shields shivered the air.

Before them stood a hill whose top belched fire and rolling smoke. Its scaly crust shone as if it hid metal. Mammon, who still walked with his head down because he had loved the golden pavement of Heaven more than God, ordered a crew of angels to dig into the hill. They picked up the spades and pickaxes they had used to build their forts in Heaven and ransacked the earth of its treasures. Soon they had opened a wide wound in the side of the hill, from which they dug out ribs of gold.

A second crew uncovered veins of liquid

fire that flowed from tunnels under the lake where precious metals were born. A third crew dug a complex mold into which flowed the molten ore.

Now from the earth rose a palace, built like a temple, set with statues and pillars overlaid with gold. The roof was wrought in gold, and the vast doors opened on row after row of starry lamps lit by oil in that skyless place. The fallen angels hurried inside, praising the architect, Mulciber, who had once made the towers of Heaven.

Trumpets announced a solemn council called by Satan in his new capital, the palace of Pandemonium. Like bees in springtime the angels crowded the porches and gates, their wings rustling, and swarmed into the great hall.

Oh, wonder of wonders! The angels, who

had once appeared as large as giants, now looked to each other no taller than elves. But deep within the inner court, the Lords of Hell, unchanged in size, sat on golden seats and made plans.

TWO

Deep in a hidden chamber sat the Lords of Hell, Moloch and Belial and Mammon and Beelzebub. From high on his throne Satan looked down at them and spoke.

"How shall we win back Heaven, through war or trickery?"

Moloch stood to answer.

"War," exclaimed Moloch. "Let's seek revenge. What can be worse than here?"

"Revenge!" shouted Belial. "How can we fight against God? What if he plunges us into flames seven times worse?"

"Why not build our own empire?" said

Mammon. "With the light from the gold and jewels we can dig from the earth, we'll imitate the light of Heaven. Who knows—we may even grow used to the fires here."

Great applause greeted Mammon's speech.

Now Beelzebub arose, majestic and grave, and his gaze silenced the others.

"Why hatch empires? The King of Heaven, who rules over Heaven and Hell, has doomed us to this dungeon. War sent us here. Let's find an easier way to escape."

That caught their attention. Now he could propose the plan Satan had suggested to him. "God has made another world, the happy home of a new race called *Human*. Though not as powerful as we are, humans are made like us. Let's learn about these creatures. Let's learn their strength and their weakness. If we can bring them to our side, God may turn against them and destroy them. Now that would interrupt his joy, wouldn't it?"

This plan pleased them all, and joy sparkled in their eyes as they voted for it.

"But whom shall we send?" demanded Beelzebub. "Who among us can cross the bottomless abyss? Who dares to fly over the sea of Chaos to find this new world? And who can hide from the angels that guard it?"

He glanced at the faces around him. All sat mute.

At last Satan rose and said, "I would not deserve this throne if fear kept me from making the attempt. And let no one go with me."

With a thunderous clamor, the angels stood up and bowed before him and praised him for putting their safety ahead of his own. The Council dissolved, and four angels lifted trumpets to their lips and blew. Now all the angels in Hell heard the news. They watched as Satan, the Emperor of Hell, shook his wings and took flight, his majestic shape growing smaller and smaller until the darkness swallowed it.

And how did the angels left behind amuse themselves while their leader was on his dangerous mission?

They played war games and sang to each other of their heroic deeds. Some explored caves where many a monster lay in wait, and passing through the bogs and dens of Hell, they shuddered at what they saw, and found no rest in this place cursed by God.

All this time Satan was flying toward the gates of Hell. On swift wings he scoured the coast, passing it sometimes on his right, sometimes on his left, as one level wing shaved the edge of Chaos, that bottomless sea.

At last he spied the nine gates of Hell: three gates of brass, three of iron, and three of rock, and all fenced with a fire that would never burn out. Before the gates sat a snaky sorceress who wore at her waist the key to Hell and whose body ended in a serpent armed with poison. Around her barked the Hounds of Hell, and at her side stood a shapeless monster who wore the likeness of a crown and shook a poison dart at the flying fiend.

"Who are you that dare block my way through these gates?" shouted Satan.

To him the monster shouted back, "Are you that traitor angel who took a third of the angels in Heaven and made war on God? Do you dare breathe defiance here where I, Death, reign as king? Back to your dungeon before I chase you with my whip of scorpions or fell you with this dart."

Satan showed no fear. Each frowned at the other like two storm clouds gathering until the snaky sorceress rushed between them.

"Oh, Father, would you raise your hand against your only Son?"

Satan drew back, astonished.

"Who are you?"

"Don't you recognize Sin, your daughter? Have you forgotten how I sprang from your head when you conspired against Heaven? I am forbidden to unlock these gates. Death will strike with his dart anyone who tries to pass."

"Believe me," said Satan, "I do not come as your enemy. I've come to free you from this dismal place. I alone dare to seek out the new world on the outskirts of Heaven. Once I've found it, I shall return for you. Death, think of it! Everything in that world shall be your prey."

Hearing that his stomach would be filled,

Death grinned. "We will follow your tracks and build a bridge over Chaos. When you return, you'll find a road that runs from Hell to the new world."

"Bring me to that new world," said Sin. From her side she took the fateful key and slid it into the keyhole, and with her hounds barking around her, she turned it.

Instantly all nine locks gave way and every bolt and bar flew out. Hinges screeched, and with a clatter like thunder, the gates moved. Hell opened like the mouth of a furnace, wide enough for an army to pass through.

Death, Sin, and Satan peered out.

Before them lay a wild abyss, a boundless ocean that roared and crashed and clattered and shrieked. All within was in confusion, as if Heaven itself were falling. Satan paused on the brink of Hell. This was no narrow channel, easy to cross. At last he spread his wings and flew into the surging smoke, which lifted him high over the abyss.

Suddenly the smoke vanished and he felt himself dropping through empty space. Ten thousand fathoms he fell, and he would be falling still if a fiery cloud had not tossed him up again. Now flying and now swimming, sinking and wading and creeping, he heard an uproar of voices ahead of him. As he flew toward them he told himself, "I will ask whoever lives in this darkness to tell me where I can find the nearest coast that borders on light."

He saw Chaos seated on his throne, beside Night, his queen.

"I am no spy," called Satan, "but a traveler, lost and without a guide. I seek the path that leads to the border of Heaven, or to some other place belonging to God. If I find it, I'll reduce it to darkness and give it to you."

"I know, stranger, who you are," rumbled Chaos. "You are the angel who led the war in Heaven. I saw the millions of victorious angels pouring out of Heaven's gates. First Hell encroached on me, and now another place called Earth hangs over my realm."

"Where is this Earth?" demanded Satan.

"It hangs from a golden chain on the side of Heaven where your army fell. If that's your path, you don't have far to go."

Satan, glad that his sea could find a shore, sprang like a flame into the wild air. He fought his way toward the first rays of morning light, which glimmered over the walls of Heaven at the edge of the abyss. Like a weather-beaten ship heading for port, he moved more easily now. Ahead of him he glimpsed the sapphire towers of Heaven.

And hanging by a golden chain, the Earth.

THREE

Now it happened that Almighty God, who sits on his high throne in Heaven, was gazing at his new creation, the Earth, where Adam and Eve, the only two human beings in the Universe, lived joyfully in the Garden of Eden. Around God flew his angels, thick as stars. On his right hand sat his only Son, who was the radiant image of his Father.

God looked toward Hell, and there in the abyss between Hell and Earth he spied Satan coasting on the edge of night, wing-weary, trying to land on the bare outer shell of the Universe. God turned to his Son and said, "See where Satan's rage has carried him. Hell cannot hold him. Now he is winging his way to the new world to see if by force or trickery he can destroy the human race."

Fragrance filled the air when God spoke, and in his Son's face shone the Father's compassion.

"When I commanded Adam and Eve not to eat from the Tree of Knowledge, I also made them free, just as I made the angels free. Human beings can choose to obey or disobey. But they will listen to Satan's lies and believe them," said God.

"Will Satan succeed?" asked his Son.

"I will give human beings a conscience to guide them," said God.

"But for their disobedience, will you destroy them?"

"All humans must die unless someone will

die for them," God answered. "Where shall we find such love? Who in all of Heaven is willing to become human and save them?"

The heavenly choir grew still, and Heaven filled up with silence. Then God's Son said, "I will leave Heaven and become a human being and let Death work his rage on me. He shall not vanquish me. I shall rise victorious and disarm him."

At these words, admiration and wonder seized all Heaven.

God turned to his Son. "You know how dear to me the humans are if to save them I must lose you for a while. Because of your goodness, you shall sit beside me. I put my angels in your charge." To his angels he gave this command: "Honor and admire my Son as you honor and adore me."

All the angels shouted for joy and Heaven

rang with Hosannas. Toward the two thrones they bowed. They cast down their crowns of gold and threw garlands of flowers picked in Paradise that covered the bright pavement like a sea of roses. After the angels tuned their glittering harps they sang praises to God and to his Son, in whose face all creatures may see God.

Meanwhile Satan set foot on the shadowy shell of the Universe and strode over the wild surface which was dark save for a distant glimmer from the wall of Heaven. No other creature, living or dead, could be found here. Alone he walked, up and down, bent on his prey, until a gleam of morning light made him turn his steps toward the wall. In the distance he saw the high gates of Heaven shining, brilliant with diamonds and gold. The golden stairs led down from the gate over a sea of liquid pearl, as if daring Satan, locked out of

Heaven, to climb them. Just under the stairs opened the wide path leading down to Earth.

How green and beautiful the new world looked! As Satan paused on the lowest step and gazed on the new world with wonder, envy seized him. But he circled, darted off, and wound his way among the stars to alight on the sun, which glowed with so dazzling a light it seemed part gold and silver, part ruby and topaz.

Looking about him, he saw an angel. Even with his back turned to Satan, the angel's brightness shimmered forth.

"Ah, here's someone I can ask to tell me where the humans live," said Satan to himself.

But first he disguised himself. He put on the form of a young cherub holding a silver wand and winged with rainbow plumes sprinkled with gold. When the angel turned,

Satan recognized the archangel Uriel, guardian of the sun and one of the seven angels who watches over the Universe for God. But Uriel did not recognize Satan, for only God can know the evil that lies invisible in the heart.

"In which shining world do the humans live?" asked Satan. "I want to see them and admire them so I can praise their Creator."

"Your wish to glorify God is worthy of praise," answered Uriel, "though coming all this way to see what others are content to hear seems excessive." He raised his hand and pointed a shining finger. "Look down on that globe. You are looking at Earth, where the humans live. That spot is Paradise, the home of Adam and Eve. You can't miss the way."

Satan bowed low to Uriel and flew off, spinning and wheeling for joy, and touched down on Earth.

FOUR

Now Satan knew that the destruction of God's creation was within his reach, but as the sun scattered its brilliance from high in the heavens, despair filled him.

"How glorious I was once! Did God deserve my hatred? Serving him was not hard. Who can I blame but myself? The more I'm admired in Hell, the more I sink into misery."

As Satan raged on, the brightness fell from his face, and Uriel who had watched him go, saw through his disguise and flew to Earth to warn Gabriel, who guarded the gates of Paradise and the Garden of Eden.

Now let me tell you about the Garden of

Eden. It lay at the top of a mountain on whose sides flourished a tangle of thickets so wild that no path brought light to the deep shade. Overhead a circle of lofty trees, cedar and pine and fir, cast shadow upon shadow. Higher still you could see the green wall of Paradise, and beyond the wall a circle of trees loaded with fragrant blossoms and golden fruit. The very air of that place would bring joy to your heart.

In the middle of the garden grew the Tree of Life and beside it the Tree of Knowledge.

Satan, supposing himself unnoticed, arrived at the border but could not find a way through the thicket. There was only one gate to Paradise, and it faced east. When Satan saw it, he chose another way. A single bound carried him over the wall, and like the wolf jumping into the sheepfold, he landed on his feet. Then he alighted on the Tree of Life and plotted the death of the two humans who lived in Eden.

How beautiful that garden was! Roses grew without thorns, purple grapes curtained the cool grottos, choirs of birds poured out their music. To the south ran a river from which rose a sapphire fountain that watered the garden as it divided into four streams. The streams ran sweet with nectar, rolling over beds of pearls and sands of gold.

Suddenly he saw them: two tall noble beings walking hand in hand, and in their faces shone the image of their Maker. Adam and Eve picked nectarines from one of the trees and sat down on a flowery bank to eat their supper. After they had eaten, they drank from the stream. Around them played all the beasts of the Earth. The lion frisked with the lamb, the bear played with the tiger and the panther. The elephant wreathed his trunk with flowers, and not far from him the serpent wove himself into an elegant knot.

"I remember the day I was created," said Eve. "I woke on a bed of flowers and wondered where and what I was. When I heard the sound of water, I followed it and lay down beside a pool. When I looked into the pool, a face looked back at me. But a voice warned me, "What you see is only your reflection that comes and goes with you. Now I will bring you to one whose image you are. And you shall be called the mother of the human race."

"To give you being, God took flesh of my flesh and bone of my bone while I slept," said Adam. "To have you by my side, I gave them from the side nearest my heart."

Eve put her arms around him, and Adam bowed his head and kissed her. Their love stabbed Satan like a needle in the heart.

"Hateful sight," whispered Satan, "these two paradised in each other's arms while I live in Hell, tormented by longing."

Down from his tree crept Satan. He entered into first one beast and then another, the better to spy on Adam and Eve. He stalked as a lion and he crouched as a tiger, watching, listening.

"The God that made us must be good," said Adam, "for he has given us all this happiness though we've done nothing to deserve it. All he asks is that we do not eat from the Tree of Knowledge. That's an easy order to follow."

Satan smiled.

"So knowledge is forbidden," he muttered. "I'll promise them knowledge that will make them as wise as God himself."

But first he would explore the garden.

Meanwhile where the rays of the sun

shone on the gate of Paradise, Gabriel sat keeping watch. Swift as a shooting star came Uriel, gliding on a sunbeam.

"Gabriel, one of the fiends has escaped from Hell to make new trouble in Heaven. Today at noon I met an angel who told me he was eager to know more of God's work. He wanted to see the Garden of Eden, so I pointed out the way. But when I caught sight of him later, on the mountain north of Eden, I saw his angry looks. Now I've lost sight of him. You must find him."

"If he leaped over these walls and is lurking here, I shall find him by tomorrow morning," Gabriel assured him.

Uriel rode the sunbeam back, and as the sun was setting, the birds and the beasts retired to their nests and grassy beds. The sky glowed with stars like living sapphires, and the moon rose and threw her silver light over the garden.

"Let sleep close our eyes," said Adam. "Tomorrow we can return to the pleasant work of pruning and caring for the trees and flowers."

"Why does the sky shine so brightly when sleep closes all eyes?" asked Eve.

"The stars rise and set so that darkness will not put out all life," said Adam. "All night long angels walk the Earth and praise God. You know how often we've heard their music at night."

At the doorway of their bower, which had been shaped by God from the most fragrant flowers, Adam and Eve praised him who made the sky, the air, the Earth, the moon, the night, the day, and Heaven itself. Then they lay down and received the gift of sleep.

While they slept, Gabriel sent angels out to look for Satan. "Let half of you fly to the south and half to the north." Then he called two of his strongest angels, Ithuriel and Zephon, and commanded them to search the garden, especially Adam and Eve's bower. "A fallen angel was seen here, bent on mischief. When you find him, seize him and bring him here."

Zephon and Ithuriel flew to the bower and found a toad squatting close to Eve's ear. Ithuriel touched it lightly with his spear. At once the toad vanished and Satan jumped up in his own shape. The two angels stepped back in amazement.

"Why are you hiding at the head of this sleeper?" demanded Zephon. "Who are you?"

"You don't know me?" sneered Satan.

"Do you think you still look radiant? You've grown as grisly as the place that sent you, and you'll give an account of yourself to the one who sent us."

Though shocked to find his brightness slipping away, Satan stood his ground. "I'll fight the sender, not the two he sent."

Gabriel heard footsteps hurrying toward him and called to his squadron of angels. "Oh, friends, I see Ithuriel and Zephon running this way and with them comes the Prince of Hell. By the look of him he will not leave without a fight. Stand firm."

When Satan faced him, Gabriel said, "Why did you come alone?"

"I alone offered to cross the abyss," said Satan, "and spy out this world, hoping to settle here or in some better place."

"Listen closely to my words," said Gabriel. "If you ever set foot or wing in these hallowed boundaries, I shall drag you, chained, back to Hell and seal you there."

"Talk of chains when I am your captive,"

sneered Satan, "but now you'll feel a heavier load from my strong arm."

The squadron hemmed him in with spears while Satan gathered all his might till his stature reached the sky. Who knows what dreadful deeds might have shaken the Universe itself if God had not hung in heaven his golden scales, the balance wherein he weighs all created things? In one pan he put the fate of his angels, in the other the fate of Satan. Satan's flew up, light as a leaf.

"Satan, I know your strength and you know mine," said Gabriel. "You can do no more than Heaven allows. See how weak your fate is, if you fight."

Satan saw and fled.

FIVE

When Adam awoke the next morning, he was surprised to find Eve still asleep, with tangled locks and burning cheeks.

"Wake up, Eve. The sun is bright on the garden, and our flowers and trees are calling us."

Eve opened her eyes, startled.

"Oh, Adam, I'm so glad to see your face. Never before have I passed a night that troubled me like this one. I dreamed a voice at my ear called me to walk out into the garden. The voice was so gentle I thought it was yours. 'Night is the cool and pleasant time,' it said, 'and all the stars have opened their eyes to see you.' I got up and went looking for you and found myself standing before the Tree of Knowledge. Oh, how much more beautiful it looked by night than by day! And as I gazed on it, an angel came out and gazed on it also and said to it, 'Oh, tree bearing divine fruit, you can make gods of humans and angels. Why are you set here if not for tasting?' He plucked the fruit; he tasted it, and horror chilled me. 'Eve, take this fruit,' said the angel, 'so that you may be a goddess.' He held the fruit to my mouth and it smelled so sweet I had to taste it. At once I found myself flying with him into the clouds. Suddenly my guide disappeared and I woke up. How glad I am that this was just a dream."

"This dream I do not like," said Adam. "But evil in a dream may come and go. In dreams we do things we would never do when awake.

Let's go to our pleasant work in the garden."

Eve felt cheered by this, though she brushed away a tear. Before they left their bower, they asked God to take away the evil that came to them during the night. When they sang their morning song of praise they invited all creatures to join them.

"You that glide in water,
And you that fly,
And you that walk
Or creep on the Earth,
Sing God's praises.

"Moon, sun, and planets,
Fogs and fountains,
Mists and winds,
Trees and flowers,
Sing God's praises."

As Adam and Eve pruned and weeded, God looked down at them with pity. Then he called Raphael.

"Go and visit Adam and Eve. Warn them. Remind them of their happiness. Tell them that Satan is plotting their fall. Tell them they are free to choose Eden's happiness or Satan's lies."

On rainbow wings Raphael flew through Heaven. The angelic choirs parted to let him pass and the gates on their golden hinges swung open for him. Down, down, he sailed, riding the winds between worlds and worlds, till he alit on the eastern cliff of Paradise and passed the glittering tents of angels standing watch. At last he came to the fragrant groves and gardens of Eden.

Seated in the doorway of his bower, Adam saw an amazing sight: an angel with two wings on his shoulders, two at his waist like a golden belt, and two sky-blue wings at his heels. He called to Eve, who was preparing a supper of delicious fruit.

"Hurry, Eve, and look at the glorious shape headed this way. Perhaps he's bringing us a message from Heaven."

"I'll make a special feast to honor our guest," said Eve. Quickly she gathered berries and nuts, grapes and apples, melons and peaches, and carried them to the grassy circle of raised turf that served as their table, which she heaped with her harvest.

Then she strewed roses on the ground in front of the bower.

As Raphael approached, Adam and Eve bowed low.

"Hail, Father and mother of all humankind," said Raphael.

"Native of Heaven," said Adam, "you honor us with your visit. Please sit in our shady bower and rest and taste the bounty of the garden—if angels can eat Earthly food."

"Adam, angels come gladly to visit you when you invite them. Though I drink dew in Heaven, do not wonder that my heavenly body can change your Earthly food to what may sustain an angel."

Raphael ate with real hunger, and Eve kept their cups filled with nectar. In those days, there was no fear lest dinner cool.

"Someday, you may visit the angels and live like them, if you are obedient to God, whose children you are," he said.

"'If you are obedient'—what does that warning mean?" asked Adam. "Can we desert God, who made us and placed us here?"

"Listen," said Raphael. "You owe your

happiness to God, but keeping your happiness is up to you. We serve God freely because we love him. You are free to choose."

"We can never forget to love our maker," said Adam. "But could you tell me something I want very much to know? What happened in Heaven before we came?"

Raphael was silent for a moment as he pondered how to tell the tale.

SIX

Long before Earth hung on a golden chain between Heaven and Hell, long before Chaos knew limits, God sat on his throne with his Son seated on his right hand and summoned his angels. From the farthest corners of Heaven they flew, tens of thousands bearing banners and flags, their hierarchies ranked in widening circles such as stones make when they're thrown into deep water.

"Angels of every rank, hear my decree. I appoint my Son as your leader. Bow to him as you would to me, and obey him as you would obey me."

All seemed pleased with this news and rejoiced on the holy hill of Heaven, dancing to the music of the planets as they turned. As evening approached, the dancers found the tables set with cups of pearl full of ruby nectar and platters of gold piled high with grapes, mangoes, figs, and melons. Crowned with flowers and seated on flowers, the angels ate and drank and praised God until twilight made their eyes heavy. All lay down to sleep, except for God, who never sleeps, and the angels assigned to sing God's praises till the darkness lifted.

Among those who did not sleep I must name one more: Lucifer, the archangel most favored by God, who was ready to burst with envy. Since the war in Heaven, he is called by a new name: Satan. The question gnawed at his brain: Why wasn't I chosen for this honor?

He nudged his companion, Beelzebub,

whose name in Heaven is no longer spoken.

"How can you sleep, my friend, after this newest decree from God? Since God has made new laws, we may—ah, but it is not safe to speak here of these plans. Call the angels who serve under me to gather at my headquarters in the north. There we'll prepare a fine reception for the Messiah, our new king."

Beelzebub did as he was told, and Satan's followers obeyed him. Remember, Adam and Eve, that before his fall, Satan shone bright as the morning star and held high rank in Heaven.

All this God watched from his holy mountain. He turned to his Son and smiled.

"An enemy is planning to set up his own kingdom in the north, equal to ours, and declare war on us. With all speed let us gather our forces."

"Father, you're right to smile at such a plan. I will conquer them with the power you've given me. What will they win but the chance to know your strength?"

Now listen closely, Adam and Eve. Satan and his angels flew through all the regions of Heaven till they came to his palace in the north quarter. Its towers were cut from diamond quarries, its wall hewed from rocks of gold. From his high throne Satan addressed his followers.

"Angels of all degrees, we're here to plan a welcome for our new Messiah and thank him for taking away all our power and authority. From now on we'll be ordered to adore not only the Father but the Son, bowing and kneeling to both of them. We were made to govern, not to serve. Will you grovel before them or find a way to live free?"

Satan gazed at the ranks of angels and listened to their attentive silence.

Suddenly Abdiel, known to everyone for his faithful service to God, jumped up and shouted, "I never expected to hear those words from you. Do you think yourself equal to God, who made you, who made all of us? Ask pardon of God and his Son before it's too late."

"Made by God, are we?" sneered Satan. "Does anyone remember being created? Did anyone see it? Can anyone remember a time when we did not exist? Why then, our power is our own. Abdiel, take these tidings to the Messiah, and fly out of here fast before we stop you."

"I'll go," said Abdiel, "but not because I'm afraid of you. What God creates he can destroy. For your disobedience, his anger will crush you like an iron rod."

And through their hostile ranks he flew, past their fierce glances, and turned his back on Satan's proud towers, which were doomed to destruction.

SEVEN

All night Abdiel flew, and when he arrived early in the morning, he saw the broad plains of Heaven blazing with chariots and fiery steeds and squadrons of angels armed for battle. His comrades welcomed him with great applause and shouts of praise.

"Among so many fallen, one held fast and came home!"

They led him to the throne of God, whose mild voice spoke from a golden cloud:

"Well done, Abdiel, servant of God. You fought the better fight. You defended the cause of truth."

Then God spoke to the archangel Michael, who commands the angelic forces, and the archangel Gabriel, second only to Michael as a warrior of God.

"Go forth and lead my angels into battle. Chase Satan and his crew to the edge of Heaven and drive them into their place of punishment, which lies open to receive their fall."

Flames awoke in the sky as a sign of God's wrath, and smoke darkened the holy hill. The high trumpet of Heaven gave a shrill call, and the armies of Heaven began their march north. Neither woods nor hills nor streams divided their ranks, for these armies trod on the air, which held them as they marched over many a province in Heaven. Far to the north the horizon bristled with spears. Now God's angels spied Satan's army, thronged with helmets and shields, hoping to take the mount of God by surprise.

My dear Adam and Eve, you must find it strange that angel should fight with angel, and stranger still that those who once met in festivals of joy to praise their creator should meet in battle. But now the shouts of battle broke forth. High in the midst of his soldiers rode Satan, armored in diamonds and gold, driving a sun-bright chariot and guarded by flaming cherubim and golden shields.

Abdiel could not stand the sight of Satan and charged him.

"Did you hope to find God's throne unguarded?" he cried. "Did you think we would join you, or fly in terror? Did you hope to conquer Almighty God, who at one blow could finish you off, even without our help?"

Satan jumped down to meet him, blow for blow.

"An army trained in feasting and singing

and praising God! You came to win a plume from me? Let's see if your heavenly singers can conquer those who fight for their freedom."

"Your followers are slaves to a leader not worthy to walk in Heaven!" shouted Abdiel. "I serve God and obey him. Take this as a greeting from me."

He raised his sword and brought it down on the crested helmet of Satan, who reeled back ten paces and sank to one knee, clutching his spear, as if a gale strong enough to move a mountain had pushed him down. Rage seized the rebel angels when they saw their leader fall and our side shouting for joy with victory so near. Michael sounded the trumpet and God's armies shouted "Hosanna to the Highest!"

Now fury stormed the air and a clamor rose such as never was heard before in Heaven: the clash of spears on armor, the clatter of

chariot wheels, the hiss of fiery darts torment-
ing the air with fire. Both sides rushed at each
other with a rage that would have shaken the
Earth to her very core, if the Earth had then
existed. For a long time victory hung in the
balance till Satan saw that the sword Michael
brandished felled whole squadrons. With his
diamond shield held high, Satan advanced
toward the archangel, who lowered his sword
and hoping to end this war, called out, "Author
of evil, these hateful acts of strife will fall
heaviest on yourself. Your works of violence
are a crime against Heaven. Take your wicked
crew to the place of evil, Hell, before my
avenging sword settles your doom."

Satan did not retreat.

"Did you hope to chase me out with
threats? We'll turn Heaven itself into Hell,
where we can live free."

Both waved their fiery swords and their raised shields blazed like two broad suns. But Michael's sword was forged for him by God, and nothing could resist its blade. It cut the sword of Satan in two and plunged into Satan's right side.

Then Satan first knew pain, and he writhed in agony as from his side streamed the liquid, clear as light, that angels bleed. From all sides his warriors ran to him, some rushing to his defense while others carried him on their shields back to his chariot at the far end of the field. There they laid him, gnashing his teeth in anguish and shame, to find himself no match for God. But his wounds soon healed, for angels can no more die from a mortal wound than air itself can perish.

Meanwhile the other angels fought hard. Gabriel's sword broke the armor of Moloch, who threatened to bind the archangel and drag him under his chariot wheels until that sword split Moloch to the waist and send him running, bellowing with pain. Uriel and Abdiel and yes, even your visitor, Raphael, slashed Satan's followers and left them mangled on the field. All the ground was strewn with split armor, overturned chariots and charioteers and fiery foaming steeds.

Night threw darkness over Heaven and silenced the din of war. Both sides made camp. Michael and his angels set cherubim with torches to keep watch and stand guard. Satan retreated far into the darkness and called his warriors to council.

"Comrades, we have been tried in battle and found worthy of glory. Though our enemies hurt us, they could not destroy us. Let us think of a more destructive weapon."

From the circle of warriors, one exclaimed, "Unless we arm ourselves against pain, we fight an unequal battle. Pain is the perfect misery. It overturns our patience, it subdues all our strength. Anyone who can invent a better defense deserves our thanks."

"I have the secret weapon that will give us the victory," said Satan. "Just under the bright surface of Heaven's ground lie minerals of deadly power. If we dig them up and ram them into hollow engines and light them, these engines will dash to pieces whatever stands in their way."

Amazed at Satan's cleverness, his followers lost no time in digging up the heavenly soil, where they found the sulphur they needed and other minerals too, which they shaped into iron balls that their cannons would fire.

EIGHT

The next morning God's angels rose at the call of the trumpet and sent scouts to look for the enemy forces. Suddenly Zophiel, the swiftest of the cherubim on guard, spied Satan's battalion moving toward them with flags unfurled and gave the alarm.

"Arm for the fight, angels, the enemy is at hand! Gird on your armor, fit your helmets, grip your shields and bear them high, for I am sure that today holds a storm of arrows barbed with fire."

As they marched forward, ready for battle, they saw Satan moving slowly toward them. His squadrons were massed in a formation that hid their secret weapon: three cannons. Satan gave the command.

"Let the troops in front part to the right and left, that all may see how we seek peace. We stand ready to receive you, if you will hear what we propose."

He ended his speech, and the right and left flanks divided and revealed what looked like three pillars with gaping mouths laid on wheels. Behind each stood a seraph, and each seraph held a reed tipped with fire. While God's angels gazed on them with amusement, the seraphs touched the engines with their reeds.

Instantly fire and smoke roared from the engines' throats, and they unleashed a hail of iron balls that struck God's warriors with such fury none could stand against them. Down they fell by thousands, angels rolling over archangels. Satan and his companions shouted with laughter.

"Why don't these proud victors come to meet us?" joked Satan. "They came on fiercely at first, and when we offered peace they changed their minds and flew off, waving wildly, overjoyed perhaps because we offered peace."

"My leader," said Belial, "I fear the terms we offered were too hard for them to understand. It seems they can't even walk upright."

What could we do but retreat? If our angels rushed forward, they would only give Satan more fuel for his laughter. Behind those engines stood other engines and other seraphs, ready to fire a second round of thunder.

So Satan and his crew scoffed at the armies of God, certain of an easy victory. But God's angels did not stand still long. Rage prompted them to a new defense. They threw down their weapons and flew to the hills of Heaven. They loosened the hills and plucked them up by their shaggy tops with all their loads of rocks and waters and woods. Terror seized the rebel angels when they saw the mountains hurled toward them. The hills buried their cannons, and pain tore at them when they felt their armor crushed into their bodies—bodies once made of light but now grown heavy from sinning. Desperate, the rebel angels too tore up the hills and hurled them, and all Heaven would have gone to ruin if God had not determined that it was now time to honor his Son by giving him the victory.

"Beloved Son, war has done what war can do. Mountains as weapons have made wild work in Heaven and put the whole Universe in danger. None but you shall end it. Ascend my chariot, guide the swift wheels. Gird on my armor, carry my sword and my bow and my arrows of thunder. Chase these sons of darkness from Heaven into the abyss."

"Father, I will put on your terror toward those you hate as I put on your mildness toward those you love. Armed with your might I'll rid Heaven of these rebels and chase them down to Hell where they will wear the chains of darkness. Then your angels will once again circle your holy mountain, singing hallelujahs and hymns of praise."

So God's Son rose from the right hand of glory where he sat, and as the third morning broke, God's chariot rushed forth like a whirlwind, flashing flames and wheels within wheels. It was drawn by the Holy Spirit but carried by four cherubim wearing wings set with eyes like thickly scattered stars. The wheels, too, were set with eyes and over the heads of the cherubim a crystal sky held the sapphire throne inlaid with amber.

On the wings of the cherubim, on the sapphire throne, rode God's Son. Beside him hung his bow and quiver that held the three-bolt thunder, and all around him rolled smoke and flames and sparkles. Ten thousand thousand angels attended him, and twenty thousand (I was told the number) chariots of God. From far off his coming shone, and the sight of the Messiah's flag surprised Michael and his warriors with joy.

At the Messiah's command, the uprooted hills returned to their places. At the sound of his voice, the hills and valleys smiled with fresh flowers.

All this Satan saw. Jealous of the Son's glory, he stood his ground, determined to win or fall

but not retreat. The Son spoke to his angels, still weary from fighting.

"Rest from battle, my angels. It is not you but me Satan envies and hates, and therefore to me God has assigned their doom. They shall have their wish, to try my strength in battle: I alone against all of them."

Suddenly the Son's face turned terrifying. The four cherubim spread their starry wings. With a roar like a flood breaking loose, the wheels of his chariot rolled as, full of wrath, he fell upon his enemies. Under his burning wheels all Heaven shook, except for the throne of God. In his right hand he grasped ten thousand thunderbolts carrying plagues, and these he threw before him.

Astonished, Satan's armies lost all courage and dropped their weapons and fled. As the Son rode over the shields and helmeted heads of those that fell, they wished for mountains to be thrown on them again, to hide them from God's wrath.

Yet the Son held back half his strength, for he did not mean to destroy them, only to root them out of Heaven. Like a herd of wild goats, they thronged before him as he drove them to the crystal wall of Heaven, which opened to show the abyss. The sight struck the rebel angels with horror and they stepped back. But a far worse fate urged them from behind, and headlong they threw themselves from Heaven into the bottomless pit.

Nine days they fell, till the fires of Hell closed over them.

When the Son turned to meet his angels, who had watched his victory in silence, they burst into songs of triumph. They shaded him, their Messiah, with palm branches as he rode through Heaven into the courts of his father, who received him where he now sits, at the right hand of God's glory.

At your request, Adam and Eve, I have revealed what is past. I have told you about the war in Heaven and the fall of those who disobeyed God. Remember that Satan envies your life and even now is plotting to trick you into disobedience so that you may share his eternal punishment. Remember the fate of those who might have stood firm. Do not listen to him.

NINE

Y ou've filled our ears with wonders," said Adam, "and we thank you for explaining these things to us. Could you tell us why God made the Earth and the sky and those moving fires, the stars?"

"I am always glad to give you knowledge that will help you praise God," said Raphael.

RAPHAEL'S TALE: HOW GOD MADE THE WORLD

After Satan's followers fell from Heaven and God's Son returned victorious, God said, "Lest Satan gloat over the angels Heaven has lost, I shall make a new world and put on it a man and a woman. From those two shall come children and grandchildren and great-grand-children; generations as numerous as the stars. When human beings have learned to live in goodness and obedience to me, Earth will be Heaven, and there will be one kingdom of joy without end. Now, my angels, go and make homes for yourselves in the spaces that the rebel angels left behind. And you, my Son, ride forth over the Deep and mark the boundaries between Heaven and Earth. All this I shall per-form through you. Speak and it shall be done."

The angels sang praises to God, whose wis-dom brought good out of evil.

So the Son rode forth, crowned with God's glory, and the wide gates of Heaven swung on their golden hinges to let him pass. He stood on the shore of Chaos and looked out over the wild waves that surged as high as mountains.

"Silence, you troubled waves," he said, "and to the Deep, peace." Then he rode far out into Chaos. In his hand he held the golden compasses prepared by God for drawing a line around the Universe and all created things, and he marked the boundary of the new world.

Darkness covered the face of the Deep, but the Spirit of God spread bright wings over it and warmed it. Soon part of the Deep pushed and pulled itself together like clay, until at last Earth hung in the newly spun air.

"Let there be light," said God, and light sprang from the Deep and crossed the air in a radiant cloud, for the sun was not yet made. And when God saw the light was good, he divided the light from the darkness, and he named the light *day* and the darkness *night*. This was the first day, evening and morning. And

God's angels touched their golden harps and sang hymns of praise.

Again God spoke.

"Let a luminous shell surround the Universe, and let it divide the waves of Chaos from the shining sea of Heaven. Let this be called the *firmament*." This was the second day, evening and morning.

Again God spoke.

"Be gathered now, you waters under Heaven, into one place, and let dry land appear."

Instantly the mountains heaved their broad backs into the clouds, and between the mountains appeared the valleys, and the water came at God's call, wave rolling after wave, and poured streams and rivers into the empty channels. God called the mountains and the plains *dry land* and the great gathering of water he called the *sea*, and he saw that it was good.

Again God spoke.

"Let the land put forth grass and flowers and herbs and trees bearing every fruit."

He had scarcely uttered these words when plants of every shape and color, grass and flowers and vines and shrubs, burst into flower and scented the air. Last of all the stately trees, jeweled with blossoms and bearing bright fruit, rose as in a dance.

Though God had not yet caused rain to fall on the Earth, a dewy mist went up and watered the ground and each plant on its green stem. So evening and morning came and went, and this was the third day.

Again God spoke.

"Let there be lights in Heaven to divide the day from the night, and let them mark the seasons and days and circling years. They shall give light to the Earth."

And God made two great lights, the greater

to rule the day, and the lesser to rule the night. He made the mighty sun's lamp and lit it, and he made the moon, whose full face borrows the sun's light, and he spangled the heavens with stars. A joyful evening and a glad morning crowned the fourth day.

Again God spoke.

"Let the waters bring forth fish, and let birds spread their wings and fly above the Earth."

And God created the great whales and all beings of the water and every kind of bird, and he saw that they were good and blessed them, saying, "Be fruitful and multiply and fill the seas and lakes and running streams."

At once the creeks and bays swarmed with shoals of fish, whose fins and shining scales flashed gold in groves of coral under the sea's green waves. The seals and dolphins wallowed and played, and the whale, swimming or sleeping on the water, looked like land jutting out of the sea.

Meanwhile, in caves and on shores, eggs hatched and fledglings soared. The eagle and stork built their nests on the cliffs and in the tops of cedars, and high over the sea, cranes rode the currents of the wind. In the woods the smaller birds leaped from branch to branch, and the nightingale tuned her song all night long. So the waters alive with fish and the air awash with birds marked evening and morning of the fifth day.

On the sixth and last day of creation, God said, "Let the Earth bring forth cattle and creeping things."

The Earth obeyed, and out of the ground climbed creatures of every kind—the leopard, the lamb, the tiger, the hippo, and the crocodile, perfect and full grown. Cattle strolled through the fields, the stag pushed his antlered head out of the ground, and the lion, pawing the Earth to free himself, sprang out and shook his mane.

From lairs and thickets and dens came the creatures, ants and beetles and bees, flying, crawling, or walking in pairs among the trees and in flocks through the pastures. If you had been there, Adam and Eve, you would have seen the mole digging his way out of the Earth and leaving little hills of dirt behind him, and the serpent gliding tall with fierce eyes yet obedient to your call. The Earth in her glory smiled on air, water, bird, beast, and fish, and rejoiced in all that swam and walked and crept and flew.

But the sixth day was not yet done. God wanted a creature who walked upright, who could govern the rest and give thanks to the Maker of all good things. To his Son he said, "Let us make humans in our image, and let them rule over the fish of the sea and the birds of the air and the beasts of the field, and over all the Earth."

So he made the first human being out of the dust of the ground, and he breathed into you, Adam, the breath of life. He filled this garden with trees, lovely to look upon, and he gave you their fruit for food, except for the one tree. From the tree whose fruit gives knowledge of good and evil you may not eat. On the day you taste that fruit, you shall die.

Morning came and evening went, and this was the sixth day. God returned to his high home in Heaven, followed by the rippling music of harps. The planets stood still to listen and the heavens rang with the song of the angels.

Open, you everlasting gates.
The great Creator made a world
where he will visit those he created.
Humans will break bread with angels
and the angels will teach them
the life that leads to Heaven.
Open, you everlasting gates.
To create is greater than to destroy.

The gates opened and God led the way back over the broad road powdered with stars that you, Adam and Eve, call the Milky Way. The sun sank below the horizon, twilight came on, and God and his Son rested from their work and blessed the seventh day. So the Sabbath was kept with music and hymns of praise. On that day you too, Adam and Eve, shall rest from your work and remember the Sabbath. Now I have answered your questions, Adam, about how this world began.

· · ·

"Stay a little," begged Adam. "While I sit with you, I seem to be in Heaven. Perhaps you would like to hear our story?"

"It's true I do not know your story. On the day you were created, Adam, I was away, bound for the gates of Hell to see that Satan did not interrupt God's work. So I shall listen to your story as eagerly as you listened to mine."

Eve bowed to the angel and said,

"I know the story well. Adam will tell it for us both. The grapes on our vines are ripe for picking, and I will work while you talk."

And she walked to the back of the bower and stopped before a vine on which purple grapes hung heavy and sweet.

T E N

ADAM'S TALE: HOW GOD MADE HUMAN BEINGS

I woke as if from a sound sleep and found myself lying on a bed of flowers, gazing with amazement straight into the sky. When I sprang up and stood on my feet, I looked around me and saw hills and valleys, woods and streams. Then I saw creatures that walked and flew. I heard the singing of birds perched on the low branches of trees, and smelled the fragrance of those trees. All the Earth smiled with fragrance and music and joy.

Then I looked at myself, limb by limb, and I ran and jumped to see what I could do. I tried to speak, and my tongue obeyed and I could name whatever I saw. But who was I, and where did I come from?

I did not know.

I asked the sun and the Earth, "Tell me, if you saw my beginning, how I came to be here. Surely I was made by some great maker. But how can I know him and how adore him?"

When no answer came, I saw down on a bed of flowers, and sleep seized me. In my dream I saw a radiant being who took me by the hand, flew with me over the fields and lakes and rivers, and led me up a wooded mountain. The top was enclosed with beautiful trees planted with walks and bowers. On each tree hung tempting fruit.

When I woke, I found the dream was real. The Divine Being appeared before me and said, "I am the Maker you looked for."

I fell on my knees before him, and he spoke again.

"This Paradise is yours to care for and to keep. You may eat freely and with a glad heart the fruit of every tree in this garden except one. The fruit that grows on the Tree of Knowledge of Good and Evil you shall not eat. This is my only command. The day you eat of that tree you will lose Paradise and go into a world of sorrow, and there you will not live forever. You will die."

Then he looked less stern and said, "Now I give you the Earth and all the creatures in it. From you they will receive their names. I have called them to appear before you, all except the fish, who cannot leave the water."

As he spoke, the birds and beasts came two by two—two blackbirds, two alligators, two kangaroos—and it was as if my tongue knew

their true names, though those names had never before been carried on a human breath. And I knew that each animal would hold that name in its heart and pass it down from generation to generation. Two by two they came. Two rats, two tree toads, two caribou—

But something was missing. I alone had no mate, no one to share the garden with, and so to the Divine Being I said, "Author of the Universe, thank you for all the goodness you have shown me. But I am lonely."

"Lonely, Adam? You have the company of all these creatures to enjoy."

"Oh, Creator of the Universe, each animal rejoices with its own kind, the lion with the lioness, the tiger with the tigress. Birds can't converse with fish, or oxen with apes. I want a companion who is my equal."

"Why, Adam," said God, "I'm alone, and I'm

content to converse with creatures inferior to me, creatures I myself brought into being."

"Lord of the Universe, you are perfect in yourself and need no other companion. I need an equal to comfort me and love me, and for me to love and comfort in return."

"Adam," said God, "your speech pleases me. You understand that you alone are made in my image. I will bring you a companion. This companion will be your helper, your other self."

Again sleep fell on me. But as in a dream I saw the Maker of the Universe stoop over my left side and take from me a rib and heal the wound with a touch. He took that rib in his hands and fashioned a human being like me, but different, a human being so beautiful it filled my heart with a new sweetness. I woke up looking for her and spied her not far off. On she came, led by the voice of her heavenly maker. Grace was in her steps, Heaven was in her eyes, and I could not keep quiet.

"Oh, Giver of all good things, here is the loveliest of all your gifts. She is bone of my bone and flesh of my flesh, and we shall be one heart and one soul."

Hearing me, she turned, and I followed her and led her to our wedding bower.

Adam ended his tale.

"She is so beautiful," said Adam, "that what seemed lovely before she came now seems plain beside her. Nature made her too beautiful."

"Don't blame nature," said Raphael. "True love should refine your thoughts. Don't let yourself be conquered by her outside beauty."

"It's not her beauty so much as her small gestures," explained Adam, "and the graceful actions and words that flow from the harmony between us."

Raphael stood up.

"The setting sun is my signal to depart. Be strong, live happy, and above all things love God, whom to love is to obey. Don't let your passion sway your judgment. The power to hold fast or to fall lies in you."

Adam too stood up, and Eve joined them, carrying a garland of grapes.

"For you," she said, and put it into Raphael's hands. "You have been kind and gentle to us. Be good and friendly still, and return often."

"Go, heavenly guest, sent from God whose goodness I adore," said Adam.

So they parted, Raphael to Heaven and Adam and Eve to their bower.

Meanwhile Satan raged and plotted. For seven nights he rode the darkness, and on the eighth night he sank into the river that flows at the foot of Paradise. Unseen by Gabriel and the angelic guards, he entered Eden, wrapped in the mist that rose from the ground near the Tree of Life.

ELEVEN

Now Satan considered which creature he might enter to hide himself. "What injustice," he muttered, "that angels should watch over such base creatures as humans."

Yet as he walked among the flowers and trees, he could not hold back his grief. "Oh, Earth, how like Heaven you are, and how joyfully I could have walked here," he cried.

Then he remembered his purpose. "My only pleasure will be to destroy this beauty. When I've destroyed Adam, I'll topple in one day what God took six days and nights to finish. And the beast I know to be the craftiest shall hide me."

Now he peered under bushes and into branches, looking for the serpent. Like a dark mist Satan crept through hedges and thickets, and at last he spied the serpent. It was sleeping peacefully, wound into a coil on the open grass, for in those days the serpent frightened nobody and carried no poison. Satan gave a deep sigh.

"The indignity of it, that I who commanded an army against God must creep into a beast."

Careful not to wake the creature, Satan entered the serpent's mouth and waited till the first light of morning broke over Eden and fragrance rose like incense from the altar of the Earth.

Adam and Eve greeted the morning with prayers, and discussed how they could best care for the garden, which had outgrown what their hands alone could do.

"The garden is running wild," said Eve. "The herbs and flowers are growing faster than we can prune and bind them. Let's divide our labors and work separately. When we work together we laugh and talk and don't finish our tasks."

"God hasn't given us such a hard task that we can't stop to talk or rest. He made us to enjoy the garden. We could work apart for a short time. But I worry about you. The enemy Raphael warned us about is probably watching us even now, trying to catch one of us alone."

"You don't believe I can stand firm? I didn't expect to hear you say that. You think I can be tricked?"

Adam put his arm around her.

"Eve, the enemy must be very clever to have persuaded so many angels to follow him out of Heaven. Don't turn away my help."

"Temptation won't hurt us!" exclaimed Eve. "Do you think God made us so weak?"

"God made us free to choose, but we could fall into a trap unaware. It's easier to avoid if we stand together. But I won't keep you here against your will."

"Then let me go alone," said Eve.

"Oh, come back quickly, Eve."

"I'll come back to the bower by noon, and we'll have lunch and take a rest."

Lurking among the cedars, pines, and palms, Satan stalked his prey, hoping to catch Eve alone. He had given up when suddenly, half hidden by the arching stems of roses, Eve appeared in a cloud of fragrance. He drew near and watched as she stooped to support this flower or bind that slender stem, and for a time he forgot his hate, envy, and revenge, and remained stupidly good, entranced by her smallest gestures.

But the hell that burned inside him

brought him back. With shining eyes he approached Eve. His head was held high, perched on his body's brilliant spirals of green woven with gold. He seemed to float, for in those days the serpent did not crawl on its belly but moved upright. Never has there been a serpent lovelier. Eve heard the rustling of leaves but paid no attention.

Bolder now, he danced before her, and bowed his crested head and sleek shining neck, and licked the ground she walked on, like an animal wanting to play. When she turned to look at him, he spoke, tuning his words to her heart.

"Do not wonder, sweet mistress of this place, that I gaze at you and adore your heavenly beauty. Who sees you here except rude beasts and one man? Oh, you should be adored as a goddess and served by angels."

"How does it happen that you can speak with a human voice? No other creature has the power of speech. And why are you so much friendlier to me than the other animals?"

"Resplendent Eve," murmured Satan, "I was once like the other beasts, and thought of nothing higher than food and sex. Until one day, roaming the fields, I noticed a splendid tree far off, laden with apples of marvelous mixed color, red and gold. When I drew nearer, a scent sweeter than I had ever known sharpened my appetite. Around the tree stood other beasts that longed to taste the fruit but could not reach the branches where it hung. I wound myself around the mossy trunk and climbed to the boughs.

"No sooner had I eaten my fill than I felt myself changed, gifted with speech and reason. I began to consider all the things in Heaven and Earth that are fair and good. But nothing I ever saw is as fair as you, whom I worship as queen of all creatures."

"Serpent, you overpraise me," said Eve. "But where does that tree grow? How far from here? Many trees unknown to us grow in Paradise, and the fruit hangs on them untouched till we have more hands to help us."

"Empress," whispered Satan, "the way is not far. If you will follow me, I'll take you to it."

"Lead on, then," said Eve.

TWELVE

Hope brightened the serpent's crest as he rolled his intricate tangles straight to the Tree of Knowledge. But when Eve saw the tree, she shook her head.

"Serpent, we might have saved ourselves coming here. Of this tree we may not taste. God commanded it. The rest he leaves to us."

"Indeed?" exclaimed Satan. "God has declared humans Lord of everything on Earth and in the air, yet he forbids you to eat the fruit of the trees?"

"We may eat the fruit of all the trees in the garden except this one," replied Eve. "God told

us, 'You shall not eat of the fruit of the Tree of Knowledge or touch it, lest you die.'"

Satan, with a show of indignation as if at some great wrong, raised his voice in an impassioned plea.

"Queen of the Universe, do not believe these threats. You shall not die. How could you? I tasted the fruit of this tree and lived to find a better life than was meant for me. Why did God forbid this if not to keep you low and ignorant, worshipping him? He knows that the day you eat of the tree, you will grow as wise as God himself."

Still Eve hesitated.

"God is just, he can't intend to harm you," coaxed Satan.

"What about death?" asked Eve.

"To die means you'll put off your humanness and become a heavenly being. Goddess, take and taste."

Eve fixed her eyes on the apples. The hour of noon drew on, and their fragrance woke her appetite. The serpent's words sounded truthful enough.

"In forbidding us this fruit," she mused, "God forbids us to be wise. But what good is wisdom if eating it dooms us to die? But the serpent didn't die. To him it brought joy. What should I fear? Here grows the fruit to make us wise. Fair to the eye, inviting to the taste, it feeds both the body and the mind."

So saying she reached. She plucked. She ate.

Earth felt the wound. A sigh ran through all creation. Back to the thicket slunk Satan and changed to his own shape, and well he might, for Eve was wholly intent on eating. She ate greedily, with no thought of God and no thought that she was eating death. Full at last, she bowed to the tree and spoke to it.

"Oh, most precious tree, henceforth I shall praise you every morning, and tend you and eat of your fruit till I grow as wise as God, who knows all things. Heaven is high; perhaps at this moment the gaze of our great forbidder is elsewhere."

Then she remembered Adam. What should she tell him? She could share her discovery or she could keep the knowledge in her power alone. But what if God was watching after all?

"What if I'm banished? Adam will marry another Eve and live happily in Eden with her. No, Adam must share my fate. I love him so dearly that with him I could endure all deaths, but without him life is nothing."

Meanwhile Adam, awaiting her return, had woven her a crown of flowers. But when she did not come back, he sensed something was wrong, and felt the beat of his heart quicken as he set off along the path she had followed that morning. Passing the Tree of Knowledge, he met her, and in her hand she carried a branch freshly picked, loaded with apples. She hurried toward him, chattering blithely.

"Did you wonder why I stayed away so long, Adam? I missed you terribly; I'll never leave your side again. But I bring wonderful news. This tree is not dangerous. The serpent ate its fruit and did not die. He gained a human voice and human sense, and he showed me why I should eat it also. So I tasted it and felt my eyes opened and myself growing up to god-head."

Adam stood amazed.

"I brought this for you, Adam. Without you, there is no happiness. You taste it, too."

A chill ran through him. Speechless and

pale, he dropped the garland as the petals faded. To himself he said, "Oh, fairest of creation, the last and best of all God's works, you are lost. The enemy has tricked you and ruined us both, for how can I live without you in these wild woods? If I gave up another rib and God made another Eve, you would never leave my heart. No, you are flesh of my flesh and bone of my bone. In bliss or in woe, we share one fate."

But to Eve he spoke more hopefully.

"A bold deed you have done, adventurous Eve. Perhaps you won't die. I can't think that God would destroy us, his prime creatures. He set us to rule over the Earth, which if we fall will also fall. Your fate will be my fate. To lose you would be to lose myself."

"In this I see the proof of your love," said Eve. "So here's to life made sweeter with new hopes and new joys. Throw your fear of death to the winds."

From the bough she picked an apple and gave it to Adam.

"On my experience, Adam, taste and eat."

Overcome with her beauty, Adam took the apple, and against his better judgment, he ate.

For the second time that day, Earth trembled and groaned. Muttering thunder, the sky darkened and wept. But Adam ate his fill. And now Eve's beauty inflamed his senses, and her eyes too darted contagious fire as he led her to their bed of flowers and they gave themselves over to passion.

When they awoke, they saw for the first time their nakedness. Covered with shame, they sat in silence until Adam found his tongue.

"Shame shows in our faces. How can I look

on God's face, or Raphael's, that I once met with joy? Cover me, you pines and cedars, and hide me where I may never see them more."

"Let's gather broad leaves," said Eve, "and stitch them together to cover ourselves."

So they went into the thickest woods and chose the smooth broad leaves of the banyan, which some call the fig tree, and with what skill they had, Adam and Eve took vines and stitched coverings to wrap around their waists. And while they stitched, they wept, and new passions rose in them: anger, hate, mistrust, and suspicion.

"What possessed you? If you had listened to me and stayed with me, we would be happy, not naked and miserable," scolded Adam.

"Was I never to leave your side and be a lifeless rib forever?"

"Ungrateful Eve!" shouted Adam. "Is this

how you show your love? What more could I have done? I warned you that the enemy lay in wait. You charmed me. You seemed so perfect I thought no evil would dare harm you. That error has become my crime, and you the accuser."

They argued back and forth, accusing each other, but neither thought to blame themselves.

THIRTEEN

Satan's deed was known in Heaven instantly, for nothing escapes All-Seeing God. From Paradise to high Heaven flew the angelic guards. Mute with sorrow, they wondered how Satan had stolen into the garden undetected. As the news spread, all the citizens of Heaven hurried to gather at God's throne and hear what had happened.

From his secret cloud, God spoke.

"Assembled angels, and you powers newly returned from your unsuccessful watch, do not be dismayed. Your care could not prevent this. Adam and Eve had free will, and nothing remains but to pass on them the sentence of mortality and death. Whom shall I send to judge the humans but you, my Son, their friend and mediator?"

"Father, my work in both Heaven and Earth is to do your will. I go to judge Adam and Eve, but I will temper justice with mercy. Through me they will see you and hear your voice. Satan is already condemned, and the serpent is not guilty."

From his radiant throne the Son rose, and angels of every rank accompanied him to Heaven's gates, from which he could see Eden and the coast of Paradise. Swiftly he flew down, down, and arrived in the cool of the evening.

Walking in the garden Adam and Eve heard God's voice. Satan heard it also from his hiding place in the woods, not far from where the two humans hid themselves among the thickest trees. Fearing what God's wrath might inflict on him, Satan fled.

God approached the forest and called out,

"Where are you, Adam and Eve, who once met me with joy? I miss you. What change keeps you absent or delays you? Come forth."

Adam stepped forward and Eve followed. Love was not in their looks, either toward God or toward each other.

"I heard you coming," said Adam, "and I was afraid."

"You have often heard my voice and not feared it," said God. "Why am I so dreadful to you now?"

"I hid myself because I am naked."

"Who told you that you are naked? Have you eaten of the tree whose fruit I said you should not eat?"

"This woman you made to be my helper, who was so good that from her hand I could suspect no ill—she gave me the fruit, and I did eat it."

"Was she your god that you obeyed her instead of me?"

Adam did not answer, and God questioned Eve.

"What is this you have done?"

"The serpent deceived me, and I did eat," whispered Eve.

When God heard this, he spoke to the serpent.

"For hiding Satan, you shall no longer walk upright but grovel on your belly all the days of your life. Adam and Eve's children and grandchildren and the generations to come shall bruise your head, and you shall bruise their heels."

Then God turned back to Adam and Eve and pronounced their punishment.

"Eve, destined to be the mother of the human race, you will bring forth children with pain and hard labor. Adam, because you obeyed your wife and not me and ate the fruit I commanded you not to eat, cursed is the ground for your sake. Thorns and thistles it will bring forth, and the sweat of your face will soak your bread until you return to the ground from which you came. Dust you are and to dust you shall both return."

Then, pitying how Adam and Eve stood before him, naked to the air that was already turning cold, God took from the sheep, the bear, the musk ox, the llama, and the goat an offering of fur, and he clothed their nakedness with warmth from the beasts.

And now God ordered his angels to change

the sweet climate of the Earth. From the north they called the terrible cold of winter; from the south they brought summer's scorching heat, and they told the thunder when to roll with terror through the darkening sky. To the winds they set four corners, and tuned them to bluster and stir up the sea and the air. Some say God ordered his angels to tip the Earth on its axis and make the seasons change. No longer did eternal spring smile on the whole Earth, no longer did light and darkness keep equal days and nights. Now Earth knew ice, snow, hail, and furious winds. Thus began the outrage against Paradise from lifeless things.

And discord among all living things followed. Beast fought with beast, and bird with bird, and fish with fish, and devoured one another. They no longer stood in awe of humans, but glared at them or fled from them.

All this Adam saw from his hiding place in the woods.

"Oh, misery! Is this the end of God's glorious new world? My children will curse me for bringing death into their lives. God, did I ask to be created? When you told me the terms, I should have refused."

That thought gave him pause.

"But what if my child disobeys me and says, 'Did I ask to be created?' No, God made me to serve him, and the punishment is fair. How gladly I would die now, rather than live knowing death will come. Death for the generations to follow—the blame lights on me. Let death take me now."

And he stretched out on the cold ground and cursed his creation. When Eve saw him so desolate, she tried to comfort him with gentle words. But he pushed her away.

"Out of my sight, you serpent. If not for you, I would still be happy. When I let you leave my side, I thought you were wise and proof against all the enemy's assaults. It was all show. You're nothing but a rib, crooked by nature, bent on mischief."

Eve fell at his feet, weeping.

"Don't forsake me, Adam. While we live let there be peace between us. I am far more miserable than you, for you only sinned against God. I have sinned against both God and you."

Adam felt his anger quieting, and he helped her to her feet.

"Let's not blame each other any longer. Love will show us how we can lighten each other's burdens. I see now that death will be no sudden end, but a slow dying to increase our pain, and our children's pain as well."

"We are childless now," said Eve, "and if we

have no children, death can only feast on two of us. Or we can cut life short and seek death ourselves—"

She broke off here, so full of despair that she could think of nothing but death. But Adam turned his mind to better hopes and saw their problem more clearly.

"If we bring death on ourselves, Satan will go free and escape his punishment. Remember how God judged us without anger? How mild he was, how graciously he spoke to us? How he pitied us and clothed us?"

Eve was silent.

"Your punishment is pain in childbirth, but afterward our children will bring us joy. As for me, I must work to earn our bread. But what harm is that? Idleness is worse. Let us pray to him and learn how to protect ourselves from rain and hail and snow and wind."

"And learn how to make fire, the way lightning does when it strikes a tree," said Eve.

"We need not fear to pass our lives comfortably enough, until we return to dust, our native home and our final rest," said Adam.

"Let us return to the place where God judged us," said Eve, "and kneel before him and beg his pardon."

And so they returned to the place, fell on their knees, and confessed their faults, watering the ground with their tears.

Far away, Satan was returning home to Hell in triumph, pleased that he would not feel his punishment until far in the future.

FOURTEEN

At the gates of Hell, which were wide open and belching flames, sat Sin and Death.

"Oh, Death," exclaimed Sin, "why do we sit idly looking at each other while our father seeks a happier home for us? He must have found one, or his avengers would have driven him back here. Death, my shadow, come with me. I feel new strength rising and wings growing. Let's build a road over Chaos that will reach from Hell to the new world Satan has conquered."

As a vulture hangs over a battlefield, eager to feast on the dead, so Death sniffed the murky air and smelled the change on Earth.

"Go," said Death, "and I'll not lag behind. I can taste the death of all things that live there."

Out they flew through the gates and hovered over the sea of Chaos, and whatever it tossed up that was solid or slimy they shoaled toward the mouth of Hell, like two polar winds driving before them mountains of ice. Death separated out the cold and dry solids for the masonry of the bridge, and with one touch of his spiky staff, he petrified them. Then he bound the stones with asphaltic slime and sealed them to stillness with a single glance.

Soon a bridge stretched over the foaming Deep that joined the shell of the Universe to Hell, following Satan's path to the spot where he first landed. With iron pins and chains they braced it, and now the foot of the stairway to Heaven and the passage leading to Earth met the new causeway to Hell.

Suddenly they spied Satan. Though he was disguised as an angel, his children recognized him. At the sight of that stupendous bridge his joy soared. For a long time he stood admiring it, till Sin broke the silence.

"Oh, Father, this is your trophy, won for your great deeds and for our freedom. In my heart, which beats in secret harmony with yours, I felt that Death and I should follow you. Now the whole world is yours. Let God divide the Universe with you or feel your strength in battle."

"This is proof that I deserve to rule the infernal empire," Satan crowed. "Your glorious work—and so near Heaven's door—makes Hell and Earth one continent. While I cross the darkness to let my legions know of my success, you two go this way, through the constellations."

He gestured toward the stars.

"It's all yours, right down to Paradise. There you can rule in bliss over the Earth and the air and the humans, whom God made Lords over all. Be sure to enslave them first and kill them last. Go, and be strong."

Free to roam, Sin and Death sped through the constellations and planets, and the poison they spread darkened them like an eclipse.

As Satan took the causeway to Hell's gates, he felt Chaos pounding and shaking the stones with rage. Passing through the unguarded gates, he found the place deserted. His angels had retired far inland to the capital, where they watched for their emperor's return. The angels that sat in council waited for news of him.

Dressed as an angel of the lowest order, Satan walked through their midst, ascended the throne, and sat down in the council chamber unseen. Then he let his glory shine forth, star-bright or brighter, clad in what false glitter was left to him since his fall. The sudden blaze astonished his followers, who joyfully rushed forward to congratulate him. Satan raised his hand for silence and addressed them.

"Powers, princedoms, angels of every rank, I return successful beyond our wildest hopes to lead you out of this infernal pit. We are now lords of a spacious world hardly inferior to Heaven. It would take too long to tell you the pain I have suffered crossing the Deep, over which Sin and Death have paved a broad road to ease your glorious march. Oh, I battled darkness and the clamorous uproar of Chaos, and I found the new world, a paradise of absolute perfection, in which God placed his new creation: humans."

Great applause greeted this account, but again Satan lifted his hand for silence.

"By trickery I made them disobey their creator, and—to increase your wonder—with an apple! For an apple God has given up his new world to Sin and Death, and so to us, to dwell in and to rule. He also judged me, or rather the serpent in whose shape I deceived them. I am to bruise their heels, and their children, not yet born, shall bruise my head. Who would not buy a world with a bruise, or even worse pain? Now nothing remains but for us to enter into bliss."

Having said this, he stood a moment, expecting shouts of triumph to fill his ears. And what did he hear? Not high applause but a dismal hiss, the sound of public scorn. He wondered why, though not for long. He felt his face draw in and his features turn sharp and spare. His arms clung to his ribs and his legs entwined each other until his body sank to the ground. He was now a monstrous serpent, crawling on his belly.

He tried to speak, but hiss answered hiss from forked tongue to forked tongue, for now all were changed to serpents. Monsters swarmed the hall and the din of hissing was dreadful. Satan, grown into a dragon, loomed larger than the rest. Still he held sway over his council. They followed him outside to the open field where the rest of the fallen angels waited, expecting to see their glorious chief stride forth in triumph. But horror fell on them, and their applause turned to hissing, for what their eyes beheld they felt themselves becoming. Down dropped their spears and shields. Their bodies changed as if by contagion.

Nearby stood a grove, newly sprung up and laden with fair fruit like that which Satan used as bait to catch Eve. Maddened with scalding thirst and fierce hunger, the serpents rolled in heaps toward the trees and climbed them, eager to gorge themselves. But instead of fruit, their jaws closed on ashes. Writhing, they spat out the bitter taste.

And still they hungered, and ate again, and spat out ashes.

Some say the rebel angels wear the shape of serpents for a certain space of days each year, to dash their pride and kill their joy in tricking Eve.

Meanwhile Sin and Death arrived in Paradise.

"Well," said Sin, "isn't this better than sitting at the dark door of Hell half starved?"

"I love best the place where I can find

enough to cram my maw," answered Death.

"You can start on these herbs and flowers," said Sin. "Feed on the beasts and birds next. Whatever time destroys is yours to devour. Wait till I have infected the actions and thoughts of all humankind. Humans will be your last and sweetest prey."

FIFTEEN

On the place of their judgment, Adam and Eve knelt and prayed for mercy. Their prayers flew straight to Heaven and passed through the heavenly doors to the golden altar, where the Son clad the prayers with incense. Then he put them in a golden censer and carried them joyfully to God's throne.

"Father, I bring the prayers of Adam and Eve, and they are more fragrant than all the trees and flowers they tended in Paradise. Listen to their sighs, for when they pray they are unskilled with words. As their advocate, let me interpret for them. Soften your sentence. Let them live out their numbered days, and after death let them live with me in joy and bliss."

"What you request is already my decree," said God. "But these two can no longer live in Paradise. The pure air of that place will eject them. Let us call to council all the blessed citizens of Heaven so they may know how I shall deal with Adam and Eve."

The Son signaled to the bright angel that kept watch, and the angel blew his trumpet. The golden blast filled all the regions of Heaven: the bowers and fountains and springs where the angels sat in joyful fellowship by the waters of life. Hearing the summons, they flew to take their seats around the throne of God.

"Oh, sons of light, since Adam and Eve tasted the forbidden fruit, they have become like us, knowing both good and evil. They would have been happier knowing only good, and evil not at all. But lest they dream of living forever and reach for the Tree of Life, they must leave Paradise at once."

A sorrowful silence held the listeners.

"Michael," said God, "take from among the cherubim your choice of warriors, lest Satan try to raise new trouble. Set them to guard the eastern gate of Eden and set a flaming sword to guard the path to the Tree of Life. Drive the sinful pair from the holy ground of Paradise to the unholy ground outside, and tell them that they and their children and their children's children are banished forever. But do not terrify them. If they obey willingly, show them what events the future will bring and send them forth, grieving, yet in peace."

In Paradise, Adam and Eve ended their prayers, and felt both hopeful and afraid.

"Eve, since we've prayed, peace has returned

to me. Remember God promised that our children will bruise our enemy? Then hail to you, mother of all humankind. Through you humans will live."

"I am not worthy of that title," said Eve, "but God's pardon must be infinite, since I who brought death on us all will be the source of life. But now our fields call us to work. Though the work will be harder, we'll live here, fallen but content."

But fate had decreed otherwise. The sky darkened as the morning sun hid in eclipse. The eagle dropped from his high nest and drove before him two bright birds, and down the hill the lion chased two deer, a hart and a hind, who fled to the eastern gate of Eden.

"Oh, Eve, I fear some further change awaits us. What else could these strange sights mean? And look—a white light is descending to meet us. Some great visitor from heaven is coming. He looks more solemn than Raphael, and less sociable."

On a hilltop the archangel paused. He wore armor, a shining military vest. His hand carried a spear, and by his side hung the sword that had wounded Satan in battle. As he drew near, Adam and Eve bowed low. Michael did not return the greeting but declared his purpose.

"Your prayers have been heard in Heaven, and God will save you from Death's claim if you repent. Your faith and your good deeds will make up for your disobedient act. But you can no longer dwell here. I have come to send you out of the garden."

Adam, chilled to the heart, was struck dumb, but Eve began to weep.

"Oh, this stroke is worse than death! Oh,

my flowers, who will care for you and water you? I tended you lovingly from bud to blossom. I gave you names. How can we leave our bower and how can we breathe other air, accustomed as we are to this—"

Michael interrupted her.

"Do not grieve, and do not set your heart on what is not yours. Your exile will not be lonely, Eve. Adam goes with you. Where he lives, that is your native land."

"Since my cries are like breath against the wind," said Adam, "I submit to God's decree. What grieves me most is knowing I shall never see his face again or worship at those places where he appeared. I can never tell my children, 'On this mountain he appeared, under this tree. I heard his voice among these pines. I talked with him beside this fountain.' Where shall I find him in the outside world?"

"Adam, God's presence is not confined to Eden. His being fills the whole Earth—the land, the sea, the air. In the valleys and plains where you will live, God is as present there as he is here. He still follows you, still surrounds you with his love. Before you leave Eden, know that God sent me to show you what will come to pass in future days."

"How can such things be shown?" asked Eve.

"By conversation and by dreams," said Michael.

With three drops of the water of life, he drenched Eve's eyes with a wise sleep. Then Adam followed him to the top of the highest hill in Paradise, and Michael put three drops into his eyes also.

"Now, Adam, see what will follow what from your fall."

SIXTEEN

Adam looked.

He saw a field, and on one part stood sheaves of newly harvested wheat, and on the other a sheepfold. A simple altar, built of sod, marked the middle of the field. There came a reaper carrying a yellow sheaf, the first fruits of his field, and he laid his offering on the altar. Then there came a shepherd carrying the choicest lamb of his flock, which he sacrificed on the altar. Fire from Heaven accepted and consumed the shepherd's offering, but not the sheaf, for the reaper did not offer it with a sincere heart. And the reaper raged and picked up a stone and struck the shepherd, who with gushing blood groaned out his soul.

"These are your sons, Adam."

"Is this death?" Adam whispered. "Is this how I must return to dust?"

"You have seen the first death of a human being. There will be others. Death comes in many shapes."

Before him Adam saw a cave, and in the cave lay people groaning and afflicted with illnesses of all kinds. Despair tended them, and Death shook his poisonous dart over them but did not strike, though the sick begged for release from their pain.

"Can the image of God in humans suffer such a hideous change?" asked Adam. "Is there no other way to die?"

"There is, if you live wisely," answered Michael, "and observe the rule of moderation in what you eat and drink. Seek nourishment, not gluttonous delight, and at the end of your life you will drop like ripe fruit into Mother Earth's lap. Old age will take your strength and your beauty. Live well and let Heaven appoint the length of your life. And now prepare for another sight."

Adam looked and saw a spacious plain of colorful tents and grazing cattle. He heard instruments that chimed melodies in the hands of their players, who moved strings and stops to make marvelous chords. He saw men melting iron at the forge, shaping knives and swords and spears.

On the other side of the hill he saw a people bent on worshipping God and praying for peace and justice. Then he saw emerge from the colorful tents a throng of beautiful women, richly dressed, dancing and singing, and the men from the hill of worshippers admired them. Each man chose for himself a woman, and they feasted to celebrate their union.

"I like this vision better," said Adam.

"Don't judge what is better by pleasure alone," warned Michael. "These are the children of your son Cain. They are inventors of the arts that polish and ornament life. Those beautiful women do not believe in God, and they draw good men away from a virtuous life. Now behold another scene."

Before a city of gates and towers, giants were fighting on a battlefield scattered with bodies and swords and dead cattle. And in this battle, if anyone spoke of right and wrong, or of truth and peace and God, soldiers seized him.

"Who are these death-dealers?" asked Adam.

"They are the children of those ill-made marriages between the virtuous men and the pleasure-loving women, where good is matched with bad. They will produce giants who admire nothing but might in battle and killing and conquering nations. Now Adam, see what punishment awaits them."

The war roared no more. All now turned to feasting and dancing and drunken brawls. Only one man, Noah, spoke out against these doings. When he saw that people were slaves to their own pleasure, he moved his tents far off, and at God's command began to build a huge boat. In one side of the boat he put a large door, and he laid in enormous provisions for both beasts and humans.

And now a wonder! Two of every beast, bird, and bug arrived and entered the ark, two by two, as God taught them. Last of all came

Noah and his wife, and their three sons and their wives, and God closed the door and locked it.

The wind rose. With black wings spreading wide, the clouds gathered under Heaven and the heavy sky darkened. The fountains of Heaven opened. Down rushed the rain till the Earth vanished, but the ark floated, tilting and rolling over the waves, which overwhelmed all other dwellings and their owners. Deep under this shoreless sea, the luxurious palaces now stabled sea monsters.

All that was left of the human race lived in a single boat.

"Let no one seek to know the future and the evils he can't prevent," cried Adam. "Will the human race end here?"

"Those who spilled blood and got fame and riches and booty in the world are lost," replied Michael. "Only one man, Noah, a Son of light in a dark age, and his family denounced their ways. They built the ark you have seen. Now watch."

Adam saw the north wind wrinkle the face of the flood as if to blow it dry. The sun gazed hot on the waves, which drew back, stealing away with soft tread.

The ark floated over a high mountain.

Noah sent out a raven to look for land. When the raven did not return, he sent a dove, who spied a green tree where her feet might perch, and returned bearing in her bill an olive leaf.

At last dry ground appeared, and Noah descended with his family and raised his hands to Heaven. Overhead an arc of light ribboned with colors shone in the sky.

"I praise God that humans shall survive,"

said Adam. "I rejoice that God forgot his anger for the sake of one good man. What are those colored streaks in Heaven? Do they bind the skirts of the clouds to hold the rain?"

"That is God's promise never again to destroy the Earth by flood. Day and night, seedtime and harvest, heat and frost shall hold to their course till out of the holy fire in God's heart comes a new heaven and a new Earth."

SEVENTEEN

Here Michael paused in his tale, between the world destroyed and the world restored, to see if Adam had questions.

"You have seen the world begin and the world end, and you have seen a second race of humans grow as from a second planting. Much more awaits you, but I see that your mortal sight is failing. Divine visions weary human sense. So I will tell you, not show you, some of those who will come after you.

"I tell you of Nimrod, a hunter who loved war. Men, not beasts, were his game, for he was a tyrant. He tried to build a tower to Heaven. But God, who visits humans unseen, stepped among the builders and gave each a different language. And Nimrod's power became a tower of confusion.

"And I tell you of Abraham, wise and just, whom God called from his father's house to follow him into a land promised to Abraham by God, and from this man will rise a mighty nation.

"And I tell you of Abraham's son, Isaac, and of his grandson, Israel, and his twelve great-grandsons who will lead your descendants into Egypt. I tell of the Pharaoh of Egypt, the tyrant who will enslave them. I tell of the plagues God will send that land, plagues of frogs and lice and flies, until the Pharaoh lets your people go. I tell of Moses and his brother Aaron, sent by God to lead them out of Egypt.

"I tell how God went before them in a cloud by day and a pillar of fire by night. I tell of how the Pharaoh chased them to the banks of the Red Sea, and how Moses touched the sea with his rod and it opened to let your people pass. I tell of how Moses touched it again when the Pharaoh tried to cross, and the waters closed over his soldiers and their chariots.

"I tell of how Moses stood on Mount Sinai and received from God the tablets engraved with the Ten Commandments, the laws by which your descendants should live.

"I tell of Jesus, the Son of God, born of a Virgin in a stable in Bethlehem. I tell of the star that proclaimed his birth and of the wise men from the East who followed it and came bearing him gifts. I tell of the shepherds who heard the news from a choir of angels and hurried to the stable."

Michael stopped, for he saw that Adam's grief had given way to joy.

"Oh, Prophet of glad tidings!" exclaimed Adam. "Now I understand how from Eve and

myself all mankind shall come. But tell me, how will God destroy Satan? When and where will the fight happen?"

"Do not dream of a duel, or local wounds to the loser's head and the victor's heel. God will win by destroying Satan's work."

"The death God's law imposed on us?" asked Adam.

"God's Son will take that on himself," replied Michael. "But he will defeat Sin and Death and confound Satan. Though his enemies kill him, he will return, for Death has no power over him, and he will take his seat again at the right hand of God and proclaim life to all who believe in him."

"But what of his followers left behind? Who will guide them?"

"The Messiah will send a comforter, a spirit to live within them and guide them, and the spirit will write on their hearts the law of faith working through love. When the time is ripe, he will destroy Satan, and from the ashes of this world will come a new earth. That earth will itself be Paradise, and a far happier place than Eden."

Adam looked so relieved that Michael hastened to add, "In this world corrupted by Satan, good will not always win, and evil will often triumph."

"But suffering for truth's sake is bravery indeed," said Adam, "and the weak can overcome the strong, I know that to obey and love God is best, and that good can overcome evil. I leave this place in peace—and well instructed."

"You have earned the highest wisdom," said Michael. "Now add good deeds to your knowledge, and faith, patience, and love. You will not mind leaving this Paradise, for you will keep a paradise in your own heart."

From the east blazed a sharp light.

"The hour of our parting has come," said Michael. "You see guards encamped on the hill and the flashing of a sword, the signal for us to go. We can no longer stay. Wake Eve. I have taught you through talking, but talking is not the only road to truth. God has taught her all this in a dream."

They walked down the hill in silence. Adam hurried to the bower where he had left Eve asleep and found her wide awake.

"I know where you went, and I knew when you would return, for God is also present in sleep. Joy will come from our sorrow. Lead on, Adam, I will not delay. You are to me all things and all places under Heaven. With you I am in Paradise, no matter where I am."

Adam was pleased but did not answer, for Michael stood near. From the other hill descended the cherubim in their bright armor, brandishing before them the sword of God, fierce as a comet. The heat that blazed from it parched the mild air around them.

Michael took our first parents by the hand and hurried them to the eastern gate and down the cliff to the plain below.

Then he disappeared.

Looking back, they saw the flaming sword waving over the gate like a torch. Some tears they shed, of course, but they soon wiped them away.

> The World was all before them, where to
>   choose
> Their place of rest, and Providence their
>   guide:
> They hand in hand with wandering steps
>   and slow,
> Through Eden took their solitary way.

A Note on Milton

John Milton was born on December 9, 1608, in London, and by the age of ten he was already a poet. In his father's house he often sat up past midnight, studying and writing poems. At fifteen he enrolled at Christ's College in Cambridge, where he excelled in Latin and Greek. He lived with his Father until 1637, studying the classics and writing poetry. From 1638 to 1639, Milton traveled. During his stay in Italy, he had the good fortune to meet the great astronomer Galileo.

Milton was not only an extraordinary poet; he was also a gifted teacher. On returning from his travels, he undertook to educate his sister's two sons, ages nine and ten. In one year's time the boys could sight-read Latin texts. After three years they had studied arithmetic, geometry, and the best of the Latin and Greek poets.

Though he was severe in his teaching, their uncle John could be informal and free in his conversation. He encouraged the boys to sing, and sing they did, as long as they were with him.

As a political activist and pamphleteer, Milton wrote in defense of the freedom of the press.

He was troubled by failing eyesight, and by 1652 he was totally blind.

He was married three times. By his third wife he had two daughters, Deborah and Mary. Skilled in languages like her Father, Deborah could read Latin, Italian, French, and Greek, and after he lost his sight she would read aloud to him. It was she who wrote down his poems for him as he dictated them. *Paradise Lost* was published in 1667, followed four years later by *Paradise Regained.*

Milton died in 1674.

A Selection of Works by John Milton

"On the Morning of Christ's Nativity"

Comus

Lycidas

"Il Penseroso"

"L'Allegro"

Paradise Lost

Paradise Regained

Samson Agonistes

Source for biographical note: *Aubrey's Brief Lives: Edited from the Original Manuscripts and with a Life of John Aubrey* by Oliver Lawson Dick. Ann Arbor, MI: The University of Michigan Press, 1957.